Happy Birthday, Daddy

Teresa Reed
Pictures by Stacey Schuett

Gullah Island

Aladdin Paperbacks

Aladdin Paperbacks
An imprint of Simon & Schuster Children's Publishing Division
1230 Avenue of the Americas
New York, New York 10020
First Aladdin Paperbacks edition, April 1996
Designed by Chani Yammer and Nancy Widdows
The text of this book was set in 17 point Syntax.
Manufactured in the United States of America
10 9 8 7 6 5 4 3 2 1
ISBN: 0-689-80396-6

Shh! Can you keep a secret? Today is Daddy's birthday and you're invited to the party.

Daddy doesn't know about the party. Don't tell him!
It's a surprise!

Mommy and the kids wait until Daddy goes out.
Now it's time to get ready. It's hard to keep a secret,
isn't it?

"Hello, Shaina. Hello, James. I've come to help with the party," says Marisol. She is carrying a big bag.

The kids show Mommy and Simeon what Marisol has brought.

"Look at all the wonderful favors," says Mommy.

Outside in the yard Binyah Binyah Pollywog sees the decorations. He croaks in delight, "Surprise!"

"Not yet, Binyah Binyah," says Mommy. "First, we have to get everything ready."

"I've made a great big birthday banner!" says James.

"Great!" says Mommy. "It's just what we need. Come on, let's get to work."

"Let's wrap our presents," says James.
Mommy helps James wrap his present. Marisol helps
Shaina wrap hers. Binyah Binyah helps everyone!

Now it's time to get into party clothes.

Shaina decides to we[ar] her favorite dress.

James doesn't know what to wear. Can you help him?

Suddenly James and Shaina hear a noise in the backyard. When they run outside, Binyah Binyah leaps from behind a tree. "Surprise!" he croaks loud and clear.

"Not yet, Binyah Binyah," says Shaina. "The party hasn't begun!"

Soon other friends from Gullah Gullah Island arrive.
James takes them outside and helps them find hiding
places. Poor Binyah Binyah can't find a good place to
hide. Can you see Binyah Binyah?

It is Shaina's job to tell everyone when her father is near the house. Finally, she sees him walking toward the front gate. "Shh! Daddy's almost here," she says.

"Surprise!" everyone shouts.
"Surprise!" croaks Binyah Binyah louder than ever.
You can shout "Surprise" too.

"Wow!" says Daddy. "I thought you forgot all about my birthday!"

Daddy blows out the candles on his birthday cake.
He saves one candle to make a wish. You can make a
wish too.

Now Daddy opens his presents. He loves the bowl Shaina made for him. He loves the nameplate made by James. It has the word "Dad" spelled out in seashells. And Marisol made Daddy a notebook for writing stories.

All evening long everyone on Gullah Gullah Island stops by to wish Daddy a happy birthday. Some people shake his hand and give him cards. Other people kiss him or give him presents. Everyone has a special birthday wish for him. You can say "Happy birthday, Daddy!" too!